**Dear Parents, Educators, and Guardians,**

Thank you for helping your child dive into this book with us. We believe in the power of books to transport readers to other worlds, expand their horizons, and help them discover cultures and experiences that may differ from their own.

We also believe that books should inspire young readers to imagine a diverse world that includes them, a world in which they can see themselves as the heroes of their own stories.

These are our hopes for all our readers. So come on. Dive into reading and explore the world with us!

From,
**Your friends at Lee & Low**

# Want to Play?

Henry   Lily   Mei   Pablo   Padma

by Paula Yoo

illustrated by Shirley Ng-Benitez

Lee & Low Books Inc.  New York

For the always playful Lucy, with much love from Auntie Paula — P.Y.

To my wonderful daughters, Sierra and Noëlle — S.N-B.

LEE & LOW BOOKS Inc., 95 Madison Avenue, New York, NY 10016
leeandlow.com
Book design by Maria Mercado
Book production by The Kids at Our House
The illustrations are rendered digitally
Manufactured in China by Imago, June 2016
Printed on paper from responsible sources
(hc) 10 9 8 7 6 5 4 3 2
(pb) 10 9 8 7 6 5 4 3 2 1
First Edition

Library of Congress Cataloging-in-Publication Data
Yoo, Paula.
Want to play? / by Paula Yoo; illustrated by Shirley Ng-Benitez. — First Edition.
     pages cm. — (Dive into reading ; 2)
Summary: "It's a sunny day and Pablo wants to play with his friends. Everyone wants to play different
things. Will they find the right game to play?"— Provided by publisher.
ISBN 978-1-62014-250-9 (hardcover : alk. paper)  ISBN 978-1-62014-259-2 (pbk. : alk. paper)
[1. Play—Fiction. 2. Hispanic Americans—Fiction.] I. Ng-Benitez, Shirley, illustrator. II. Title.
PZ7.Y8156Wan 2016          [Fic]—dc23          2015029155

# Contents

A Sunny Day          4

Want to Play?        10

Explorers            20

# A Sunny Day

Pablo liked to read books.
He liked to read books in English
and Spanish.

His sisters liked to play games.
But sometimes they were too loud.
Pablo could not read!

Pablo went outside to read.
It was nice and sunny outside.

Pablo closed his book.
Pablo wanted to play!

"Hi, Pablo," said Lily.
"Do you want to play
in the park?"
"Yes," said Pablo.
"Let me tell my dad."

Pablo put away his book.
Then they walked to the park.

# Want to Play?

Padma and Mei were
on the swings.
"Hi," said Mei.
"Want to play on the swings?"

"Yes," said Lily and Pablo.

"I feel like I'm flying!"
said Pablo.

A ball rolled near them.
Henry ran after the ball.
"Want to play basketball?"
asked Henry.

Pablo tossed the ball to Mei.
Mei tossed the ball into the basket.

Then Henry got the ball.
He tossed the ball to Padma.
But the ball went over her head.

"Let's play something else,"
said Padma.
"Want to play follow the leader?"
"Yes. We'll follow you," said Mei.

Padma climbed up the steps
of the playhouse.
Everyone climbed up too.

Padma ran to the merry-go-round.
Everyone climbed onto
the merry-go-round.
Padma made it spin very fast.

Lily felt dizzy.
"What else can we play?"
asked Lily.

# Explorers

Pablo thought about the games his sisters played.

"Let's play pretend," said Pablo.
"We can be explorers!"

Pablo ran to the slide.
"Let's pretend the slide
is a mountain," said Pablo.

Everyone climbed up the slide.
"The mountain is covered
with snow," said Mei.
"It's so cold here!" said Pablo.

Padma ran to the sandbox.
"Let's pretend the sandbox
is the beach," said Padma.

Everyone climbed into the sandbox.
"I see seashells," said Henry.
"We can hear ocean waves,"
said Lily.

Lily ran to the playhouse.
"Let's pretend the playhouse
is a cave," said Lily.

Everyone climbed under the playhouse.
"Look!" said Padma.
She picked up a stick.
"It looks like an old bone," said Lily.

Mei ran to the merry-go-round.
"Let's pretend the merry-go-round
is a spaceship," said Mei.

Everyone climbed onto
the merry-go-round.
"We are in space," said Lily.
"I see the moon," said Pablo.
"It is so bright!"

Clouds covered the sun.
"It's going to rain," said Pablo.
"Where can we play now?"
asked Padma.

"Let's go to my house,"
said Pablo.
"My sisters play lots of games.
It's always fun there!"

# Have more fun with this book!

☆ Pablo likes to read. Write a letter to Pablo. Tell him about one of your favorite books. Why do you think he would like this book?

☆ What are your favorite things to do with your friends? Draw pictures of yourself and your friends doing some of your favorite things.

☆ Do you like to play pretend? Pretend to be an explorer. Where would you go exploring? Why?

**Paula Yoo** is an author and a screenwriter whose children's books have been recognized by the International Literacy Association, the Texas Bluebonnet Award Masterlist, and Lee & Low's New Voices Award. She and her husband live in Los Angeles, California.

**Shirley Ng-Benitez** creates illustrations with watercolor, gouache, pencil, and digital techniques. She also loves to create 3-D creatures from clay and fabric. She lives in the Bay Area of California with her husband, their two daughters, and their pup.

# Read More About Pablo and His Friends!